We're a Family

written by Sandra Brandon

illustrated by Helen Endres

Library of Congress Catalog Card No. 85-62958
© 1986. The STANDARD PUBLISHING Company, Cincinnati, Ohio
Division of STANDEX INTERNATIONAL Corporation. Printed in U.S.A.

Hi! My name is Stephen. I am the oldest in my family and the only boy. I have brown hair like my mother, and I am tall like my daddy.

This is my sister Kelly. She also has brown hair like Mother. Everyone says she looks just like my mother.

This is my little sister Sara. She does not look like Mother or Dad, but Sara belongs to our family.

Sara has brown skin and black hair, and her eyes are very dark and have a different shape.

But even though Sara looks different, she belongs. She is a part of our family.

Mother shows me pictures of when I was a baby one day old! I was so tiny! And we have some pictures of Kelly one day old. We were born in a hospital, and Mother and Dad were our parents.

But my sister Sara was born in a different country. When she was eight months old, she came on an airplane. She did not have a Mother or Dad to take care of her. We all went to the airport to get her and bring her home.

There are lots of ways Sara is like me and
Kelly. She likes picnics, ice cream cones,
and merry-go-rounds.

She likes to visit Grandpa's farm and ride
on the tractor, just like I do.

Sometimes Mother takes Kelly and Sara and me to the park to play. Sara runs and plays and laughs. One day when I was playing in a fort with some other boys, Sara shouted to me, "Brother, please come swing me."

"Is she your sister?" the other boys asked. I know they asked that because Sara's skin is so brown and she looks different.

I am happy to tell them that Sara is my adopted sister, and that she belongs.

I don't want anyone to hurt Sara's feelings or make fun of her because she's different. We are all different in many ways. Some of us have red hair, some black; some are tall and some short; some have fair skin and some have brown.

God planned it that way. He made us all different, and we are all special.

Not only does Sara belong to Mother and Dad and Kelly and me, she belongs to Grandma and Grandpa and our uncles, aunts, and cousins. They are all glad that Sara belongs to our family.

Grandma always sends Sara birthday cards just like she sends them to Kelly and me.

My aunt Susan always makes me, Kelly,
and Sara new pajamas each Christmas.

Mother and Dad tell Sara, Kelly, and me that they love us all. We all belong to our family and we are all needed.

Sometimes my sisters really bother me! When I'm reading one of my favorite books, they can be so noisy! Sara sometimes loses the marker in my book and that makes me mad.

But, I am still glad she belongs to our family. Sara is happy she belongs to our family, too.

We all like to go to Sunday school where we learn about God and how much He loves us.

Here is Sara's favorite song:
Jesus loves the little children,
All the children of the world.
Red and yellow, black and white,
They are precious in His sight.
Jesus loves the little children of the
world.

I guess that song is about Sara, too. Sara belongs to our family and we all belong to God.